THE BRIDE OF THE BLUE WIND

THE SISTERS AVRAMAPUL BOOK ONE

VICTORIA GODDARD

The Bride of the Blue Wind

Victoria Goddard

Copyright © 2015 by Victoria Goddard
Published February 2017 by Underhill Books.
All rights reserved.

ISBN: 978-0-9950270-4-6

Cover Design: Victoria Goddard

This is a work of fiction.
All of the characters portrayed in this novel are either products of the author's
imagination or are used fictitiously.

1

Aldizar aq Naarun aq Lo of the city of Rin had three daughters, which would ordinarily have earned him much good-natured chaffing from his compatriots and clansmen, but because the mother of his children was Lonar Avramapul the Bandit Queen of the Oclaresh, he was instead much congratulated.

Their first daughter was beautiful and strong as a lioness, and they named her Arzu-aldizarin, and she sat at her mother's knee and learned the ways of war.

The second daughter was beautiful and sharp-taloned as a falcon on the wind, and they named her Paliammë-ivanar. She was the delight in her father's eye; he was an artist who had come to the desert to sculpt the Bandit Queen, and had never left, and he hoped she might follow his trade.

The third daughter was as beautiful and even-tempered as the moon over the desert, and they called her Sardeet-savarel. She was beloved all of all her clan, for she laughed and sang and broke hearts that mended quickly.

Each of them beautiful, each of them wise, each of them beloved. Arzu the lioness, Pali the falcon, Sardeet the moon; as they grew in stature, in the songs of the hinterlands of

Oclaresh people began to murmur of the bride-prices they would expect, and that no ordinary man could ever hope to pay.

So say the stories.

~

At fourteen Arzu left, as was the way of her mother's people, to spend a week in the desert and seek what messages the Wind Lords would send her. She went dressed in bridal scarlet with gold coins braided into her black hair, for it was said that the Wind Lords sometimes chose one for bride or husband; it was considered an honour beyond merit or questioning, for the one so chosen would become as a god in the Halls of the Sky, the palace in the heart of the Desert of Kaph where the gods ruled the world with wills fickle as the wind. One did not return from the Halls of the Sky a living man or woman, although sometimes those left behind would be granted a vision and the new name given to the one once their own, and a new deity would be inscribed in the stele of the clan gods.

When Arzu returned she went to her father and her mother and her two sisters and kissed them, and asked for their blessings, for she had had a vision of magic in knots and thread, and would go to those who made the carpets in the mountains to the south of the Desert of Kaph, and return to the clan a shaman of power.

She was given as her dowry for the carpet weavers a set of chess pieces carved out of jade by a master in a far-off land. Her father gave her small figurines of each of her sisters, and letters for the master weavers, who would recognize in his name an artist of high renown. Her sisters gave her an ivory dagger and a jade stone with a hole in its centre that Sardeet had found one day in the oasis.

Arzu rode off into the desert on her fine white horse, a

short sword on her hip and a quiver on her back, and it was murmured that if she returned she would be the next Queen of the Oclaresh.

At fourteen Pali spent a week in the desert, and when she returned she kissed her father and her mother, and her sister who remained at home, and asked for their blessings, for she had seen great wonders in her visions that she would not describe, save that a sword was in her hand for each of them. To Arzu in a letter she confided that she had seen lands beyond her imagination, mirages that she walked in, unafraid and laughing, and had learned the joy of battle.

Arzu replied that she had learned how to knot two winds together to create a thread that remembered the sky and yearned to be dyed like a bird, and that she had enchanted the statuettes their father had carved to warn her of any danger that might befall her sisters. And she sent to Pali as a gift a bright blue silk scarf from far away across the desert, and her first knotted square, which when Pali unwrapped it in her tent fluttered around like a bird. Sardeet gave her three stones she'd found in the desert, a pink flower-crystal, a grey stone singing with opal on its broken side, and a piece of fool's gold.

By her parents Pali was given the heirloom of her mother's house, the sword that would win her dowry for her, and the promise of horses and camels for when she returned. Her father gave two statuettes of her sisters; her mother, a golden hair-comb she had taken from the head of the great Andariin herself, when the Bandit Queen of the Oclaresh fought against the djinn for her territory, and won.

Pali rode out on her dapple-grey horse, with a white falcon on her wrist and a bow at her back, the sword muffled in cloth as befit an apprentice, and set off the same direction

Arzu had taken, but she turned north when she reached the mountains instead of south, and found her way to the high valleys where the Warriors of the Mountains trained in their veils.

People said she had the light of the old legends on her, and that if when she returned she called the clans under one banner they would come.

~

Sardeet was the youngest by three years, and deeply impatient for her journey to the desert and her own vision. She had blossomed young, as they said, and grew in beauty each day, until the murmurs said her bride-price would be the highest any had seen in an age, for her beauty was growing beyond compare.

When at last her turn came, she went to the desert in the due season, prepared a fire and drank the tea the oldest woman of the clan had given her, and prepared herself for the seven-day vigil. She bore nothing but her bridal-clothes, and a flask containing the tears of a god, which her mother had wrested from a caravan of holy men beset by ifrits and ghouls, and which her father had given her as protection against a fear he would not name.

On the first day, she saw a horse thunder across the sky, dapple-grey as her sister Pali's, with hooves of shining silver and an eye bright as a star. He bore a rider, a man of dark skin and flowing white garments, weaponless, unveiled, and trailing power like broken chains behind him.

On the second day, she saw something like a desert made of lapis lazuli, with a glitter and a motion to it that she'd never imagined. There was a creature on it, like a caparisoned horse with a palanquin, plunging through the blue sand with white grains leaping about it.

On the third day, she saw an oasis of trees bigger than

even in the stories, huge trees as big as mountains, and winding between them a small party of riders, like her father's statuettes at the feet of the trees. One of them wore a warrior's veils, and one of them wore a bride's scarlet, and the rest were strangers; their horses' livery was fantastic to her eyes.

On the fourth day, she saw the Moon, walking to and fro in a silver palace, shaped like a woman, her dress the colour of earthshine.

On the fifth day, a huge eagle came down and picked her up, and carried her away with him to the mountains due east of the desert, and placed her on a flat terrace built of stone before a palace built all of glass, at the feet of a man dressed all in blue.

"You are as beautiful as the winds have told me," he said, smiling at her. She saw that his beard was dyed with indigo, oiled and perfumed, scented with frankincense, and that his eyes were black and expressionless as the eagle's.

Sardeet knew the stories of the Wind Lords taking their brides from amongst those seeking visions; also she had been receiving compliments of that sort from strange gentlemen since she was nine, and she knew how to smile graciously.

"You are very kind, holy one."

He reached down one hand. His nails were clean and filed round and smooth, and he wore three rings on his right hand: an iron one in the shape of a serpent, a silver one with a single black stone set in the band, and a gold one set with a lapis lazuli signet. She accepted his gesture and let him pull her upright.

He looked her over with a deep intensity, from her crown of black hair braided up with ribbons and coins, down the flaring layers of scarlet embroidered with gold that she had spent a year and a half making for this her vision-quest, to her bare feet with her toenails painted gold —which was her own doing. His eyes were cold but gleaming, and Sardeet felt a strong ripple of desire run through her.

"Yes. You are worthy."

No one, in the stories, was given a choice. But Sardeet said, "Might this one know your name?" For she had loved those stories, and did not know of any that told of a Wind Lord who lived alone in a house all of blue glass; and the eagle had not taken her all the way into the heart of the Great Desert; and her mother was, after all, the Bandit Queen of the Oclaresh, and Sardeet was her daughter through and through.

"There are three rules in my house," he said. "One: You will have keys for all the doors in my house, but the stone door may not be opened. Two: You will have all you desire, but a door out. And three: You may ask me any question, but each answer I give shall exact of you a day's silence. Do you understand me?"

"Yes," she replied.

"Come," he said, and off-handedly, "you may call me Olu-olurin," and he chuckled. She did not make any comment that it sounded a woman's name; who knew what the Wind Lords were in their essence? Instead she felt all sounds she made disappear, so she walked through the blue glass door silent as one of the dead.

Inside the palace all was glass. The air was cool and in constant motion, and she heard whispers on the edge of hearing, though she saw no one. He led her to a room containing a round glass well, big enough for her to sit in, and with a casual flick of his hand he summoned a silvery-glinting wind, and said: "This is your new mistress."

He left her to the wind's ministrations. The wind plucked at her clothing and hair until she removed her garments and ribbons, shoved her into the water, where she discovered the delights of bathing in plenty of warm clean water scented with flowers. The wind washed her hair and dried it for her, and rebraided it so that when she was presented in front of a piece of glass with a silver backing—a mirror, she realized, though she'd never seen one so large, only the hand-sized ones her mother sometimes captured from foolish traders— she stood in front of it every inch a bride fit for a Wind Lord. Clean, scented, beautiful, her scarlet and gold the only colour besides blue as far as her eye could see.

The wind opened a door for her, and she walked through the blue glass halls, her feet still bare, until she came to a room where a feast was laid out, though there was no one there but she and her bridegroom, who smiled at her with an expression that was not human.

And thus it was that Sardeet-savarel became the seventh bride of Olu-olurin.

2

Four years after she had left to go to the southern mountains, Arzu-aldizarin left the weavers with skills and carpets enough to make her a rich woman. She rode her white horse with an unaccustomed seat, for it had been long and long—four years, in fact—since she had last ridden more than an hour or two.

At the place where the road from the southern mountains met the road from the north, she saw there waiting a person on a dapple-grey horse, dressed in the black veils of a Warrior of the Mountains, sitting with absolute ease and patience.

Arzu reined up and looked at the familiar eyes crinkling above the unfamiliar black veils, and said: "I hope you have not been waiting long?"

"Two days only," said Pali, and her voice was calmer and lower than it had been.

"I have not been riding long of late," said Arzu apologetically, and both sisters laughed and embraced, and then looked at the fourth way from the crossroads, where the road went straight east, lined with the tombs of the dead.

Their mother did not believe in sullying her hand or her

head with the written word, preferring the oral histories that had been passed down mother to daughter since the Desert of Kaph had been a garden, but their father was from the city, and he had written, with tears spotting the papyrus, that their sister had been taken by the Wind Lords on her vision quest. No one was surprised, for though it had been many years—two generations at least—since anyone had been taken from their clan or their neighbours', Sardeet's beauty was certainly enough to win the attention of the gods.

Arzu had wept, and knotted a carpet of such power that her teachers had placed it for safe-keeping in the temple sanctuary lest any try to ride it, and be carried to their certain grief. She had then sought to become an artist of such surpassing skill that she could in good conscience submit one of her carpets to the next offering to the Wind Lords, which occurred once every twelve years, and when Sardeet might condescend to accept it from her throne of glory. She also knotted a bridal crown of scarlet for Sardeet's statuette, which seemed to smile with a holy serenity when Arzu looked upon it.

Pali had performed the full ritual of mourning that the Warriors practised for their dead, seven days in meditation, seven days in prayer, seven days in fasting, and on the one-and-twentieth day released the white falcon to bear her longing into the quiet oblivion of the desert, and let her heart be at peace. Whether this had worked or not no one among the Warriors well knew, for Pali was not one to speak her heart. Like her sister, like their mother when their grand-mother died, Pali abandoned herself to her vocation, and so it was that she had taken the first of the veils a full year early.

The ceremony of the First Veil had taken place in the new moon of the seventh month, and on the full moon, by the custom of the Warriors of the Mountain, Pali was supposed to set off unarmed on a quest to find, and right, an injustice, before she could return and be granted her sword in the ceremony of the Second Veil.

On the quarter moon, while she was praying for a sign for her direction, a tiny square of carpet dropped out of the sky before her. Its pattern was in the form of three red flowers connected by a convoluted ribbon of the same colour—the ancient sign for *blood of my blood in need.*

Thus it was that Pali rode south to meet her sister.

Arzu and Pali embraced, dismounted from their horses, embraced again, and set up camp on the human side of the crossroads. Pali tended the horses and built the fire; Arzu laid out the travelling carpets and the food she had brought. They ate, chatting of little things since their last letters to each other, and only when Arzu had put on water to boil for the *slaurigh* did Pali say, "And what is it that calls blood to blood, sister of my heart?"

"For four years the statuette our father gave of you has smiled," began Arzu, pulling out two bundles wrapped in silk and unwinding the bright blue silk from one to show the carved face of Pali. "Occasionally a shadow has fallen upon it, but, I think, you have told me those things."

"I expect so," said Pali, whose reticence among strangers was released in writing to her older sister.

Arzu placed the second bundle on the carpet before them, but did not unwrap it. It was wrapped in indigo silk, embroidered in gold and silver.

"For three years the statuette of our younger sister smiled —" It was not considered appropriate, nor wise, to name one who had been taken by the Wind Lords, not until the name given to the new immortal was revealed—"and by our father's art grown with her age."

"It is so," said Pali, thinking that it was mostly due to

Arzu's own gifts; hers had not changed so dramatically, though Arzu before her was not so unfamiliar as the four years between fourteen and eighteen might have made.

"One year ago, when she was … taken, it seemed to have become … splendid. Her expression … enamoured. I knotted a bridal crown, and prayed."

"I sent my grief by a white falcon," said Pali, though she had already written to Arzu of this.

"One month ago," Arzu said, "I turned to give the new-moon prayers before my household shrine, and I saw … this."

She unwrapped the indigo cloth, and Pali had to bite back a cry—that was not considered a good attribute in a Warrior of the Mountain—at the shadowed face of their younger sister.

"I see," said Pali, and they both looked into the shadows, to the east where the night had already fallen on the gap between the mountains that led into the heart of the Desert of Kaph.

The sisters were silent for a long while. The horses moved on the grass, making the occasional clicking noise as tooth met tooth or hoof touched stone. The fire crackled in homely gold and red. And then Pali said, thoughtfully, "I am seeking an injustice to right, that I may prove myself worthy of the second veil and my sword."

She had left on her veils, but Arzu could see from her eyes that she was smiling, and in some small embarrassment of her own desires and ambitions and ancient taboos, she said, "The sword you seek to earn is one of great renown."

Pali nodded judiciously. "It is permitted to have a guide."

"The first mastery I have attained; the second is rarer, and requires one to win a new pattern."

"The heart of the desert," said Pali, "is the source of the wind."

And so the next morning the sisters rode east to enquire of

the gods what wrong was done to their sister, that she cried marble tears of anguish.

~

In the palace of blue glass, Sardeet had spent many days silent: but she had also learned many things.

She had learned that there were one hundred and forty-four kinds of spirits, and how to command the lowest six.

She had learned that there were other worlds, and that in certain places, by certain rituals, and at certain times, one could pass through the veils between worlds, and perhaps even return; and she learned twelve such passages, though her husband laughed to answer her, for her beauty was made immortal in time at the cost of its circumscription in space.

She learned that many, but not all, of the old stories held truth.

She learned other things. That the food came from the gift-offerings of a hundred tribes, brought there by her lord's little winds. That the eagle was one of a dozen, proud and great, the guardians of the Black Mountains. That the Wind Lords rarely consulted with each other, each having his or her own jurisdiction, and that the Twelve Lords of the Great Winds were the only ones who lived in the centre of the Desert of Kaph as the stories told.

She was lazy and a little curious, and—youngest and fairest of her clan—rather spoiled, and she delighted in rich things. Silent or speaking, she was attended by the silver wind and by two djinn of a lower order whom she learned to order with gestures and will. They brought her clothes, foods, delicacies, music—one djinni could sing—and most of the time she revelled in the luxuries of the palace of blue glass.

It took some months before she quite recovered her head from the sheer profusion of delights. True to his word, her husband gave her his keys, answered her questions, and fulfilled every desire of hers except for the door out. He seemed to take pleasure in her in-turning, as she began to learn the bounds of her prison. He made no effort to threaten her; he didn't need to. He did not try to enchant her into loving him, for it had been a long time since he had been human himself, and he did not remember anything but the passions; and those he was happy to fulfill.

She had not been raised to idleness, and one day when she had asked three questions in a row about the passages between worlds Olu-olurin sent her away with a laugh and a caress and three days of silence before her. He was busy with some project of his own, which she did not dare ask him about, being sure that a day of silence would not be the only repercussion of the answering.

It was early, and the thoughts of doors between worlds excited her, and she was otherwise bored with the now-familiar luxuries, and so she took up the keys of the palace of glass and began trying to match each with a door.

This was not so easy as it at first seemed, for though the palace had very many rooms, most of them had no locks. There were seventy-seven keys on the ring, from ones made of iron longer than her hand to a tiny golden key barely the length of the first joint of her thumb. It took her some weeks to find all the locks.

She found Olu-olurin's treasure room, which distracted her for a short while, but her eye had grown satiated and she no longer wondered at riches however grand.

She found a back door into his study, where he sat beside a wall where six magic cloaks hung by their necks. He smiled at her with a glint of amusement and something that made her shiver a little and kiss him, until he laughed and sent her away with six days of silence for explaining the purpose of the six cloaks. She found a door onto a platform on the tallest tower, and that nearly stopped her from further exploration, for with the free winds in her hair she felt a stirring of old desire.

The palace from above looked like the desert rose she had found as a little girl and given her sister Pali when she went into the mountains to become a warrior, only blue instead of gypsum-pink. Sardeet looked long out past the bounds of her world.

The palace sat on a ridge at the edge of the mountains; the golden desert stretched east as far as the eye could see. Even as Sardeet watched she saw the mirages begin, the desert djinn—now she knew what to look for, could begin to name them—jousting with each other in sandstorms and whirl-winds, a ring of false visions around the centre where the keenest-eyed lived, the Lords of the Twelve Winds.

West, north, south, the mountains were black and bare and precipitous. Below her the palace spread out like a flower, humming with rainbows and bound winds, with the half-invisible spirits of fire and air Olu-olurin had bound to him. That was no door out: if she jumped she would not land; she would be caught.

It did not, in fact, occur to her to jump.

At last the only key whose lock she had not found, whose secrets she had not ferreted out, was the little golden key. By this time she had passed several more periods of silence and speech—her only true measure of time's passage apart from her monthly cycles, which had grown far more irregular than they had been in world-without (as she called it to herself), and which gave her three days of absence from her husband's bed; which was a trial to her, for if he did not waste love he certainly abounded in passion.

She searched the whole palace three times over for the lock the key might fit. She did not ask Olu-olurin where it was; this was the closest thing to her own she had, and she treasured the careful hunt to assuage her curiosity. The periods of silence did nothing to reduce her curiosity, which seemed to burn clearer and stronger in her as the days passed. Olu-olurin watched her come and go with a smile on his face that was not a human smile, but she had already begun to learn what she might lose in her passage to divinity, and she did not question or fear him for the predatory glint to his expression.

She feared very little, did Sardeet-savarel.

3

Pali and Arzu took the road of the dead into the mountains.

The tribesmen of the Middle Desert—rarely those of the cities, who were afraid of the nomads, and built tombs on the eastern roads out of their habitations instead of coming this far into the desert—brought their dead to this path, which led towards the only pass through the mountains to the holy desert.

Those who died well were built tombs; those who died in sin were left to be made clean by the desert scavengers. Some tombs were mere cairns of rocks, others more elaborate dressed-stone monuments. All of them with open doors, that the spirits might come and go as they pleased. All the skeletons with white threads knotted about them, that their bodies might not.

The road went due east, lined with bones. Their horses stepped along smoothly through three days of the dead, until suddenly they reached the Gate of the Mountains, and the first of the guardians of the way.

This was a sphinx, tawny as a lioness, her eyes milky

blind, her talons brown with old blood. The bones about her feet had no look of rest; they were scattered.

Their horses were fearful but superbly trained, and Arzu's white mare took comfort from the dapple-grey's calm interest. The sisters rode at a slow walk up to the sphinx, who sat directly in the way. Wings arched up and blocked the pass from sight as well as passage; the feathers were tawny and gold and brown as a desert partridge.

Pali and Arzu looked to each other, and then Arzu dismounted and went to bow before the sphinx, which was smiling.

"Mother of gods," said Arzu, "we are two sisters seeking our sister, and we beg that we may pass you by."

The sphinx was very still, except that tip of her lion's tail flicked beside her. Then she said, "Daughters of the middle desert, this is a gate for the gods and the dead."

Arzu bowed again, and drew forth a long scarlet thread, and a white one, and one of gold, and while the blind sphinx seemed to watch, she knotted them together, hands outstretched before her, her long embroidered robes shushing as she moved.

"Mother of gods," said she, when the threads had formed an intricate circlet, the three strands tightly knotted together; to Pali's eyes it looked something like the message Arzu had sent her and something like the bridal crown and something like the glinting white strands used to bind the dead they had passed. Arzu held up the circlet. "Mother of gods, which knot is that which joins these three threads?"

The sphinx bent her head down. Her breath puffed across them, warm as a summer wind and meaty. The horses moved restlessly, and Arzu's white pulled hard against the reins Pali held in her hand.

"Daughters of the desert," she said, "you may pass."

And she lifted up one wing, so that behind the golden body they saw the golden desert. Pali dismounted and made her warrior's bow to the sphinx, and then she and Arzu walked through the narrows between the sphinx and the stone, and the horses trembled along behind them.

~

Sardeet had asked and been answered five more questions, and in the silence of the third day of these Olu-olurin came to her in the evening, and said: "New life has quickened within you. Good."

And he bade her drink from the flask of divine tears she had brought into the desert with her. She could only swallow the tiniest mouthful; it was fire all the way down.

"Each day," he said to her, "you will drink again, that our child will be born free of mortal impurity."

~

At camp that evening Pali took the circlet of knots and asked what the answer was.

"We are human beings," Arzu said. She touched the scarlet thread. "Made of flesh and blood, mortal, animal." She touched the golden thread. "Made of spirit, soul, fire from the flame at the heart of the world, immortal." And she touched the white thread, which bound the other two together. "And, mystery of mysteries to the gods who come of nature, we can take the mortal with us into immortality, by our art, by our will, by our love."

~

Sardeet had thought the tears would become easier to swallow over time: but although she could feel her body changing over the days that followed, the pain grew no less. Each morning after her bath she stood before the great mirror while her attendant djinni robed her, and stared at the fire kindled in her belly.

Olu-olurin was more attentive than before, and fed her delicacies with his own hands. Strange foods, she knew, and some things designed to give gifts to this half-divine child. He sent his servant winds out into the desert to bring back treasures: something like sugar, except for the way that it continued to sparkle in her blood; something like *slaurigh*, except that when she drank it she felt drowsy with power running through her veins to the throbbing being taking form in her womb.

She was not sick, as she had seen older cousins be sick with their pregnancies. She found her passions pouring into the fire; she could not think of it as a child, not when she stood each morning before the great mirror and saw it glowing like a burgeoning sun.

The pass through the mountains was straight, and far ahead they could see the golden desert, but before they reached there they came to the mouth of a cave.

The road passed directly in. Far on the other side, like a window—both had seen windows in the mountain fastnesses of their orders—they could see the sand golden in the morning.

They could also see that the road did not go straight across, but steeply down, and that there was a steep uphill on the other side leading to the sun.

"Twelve days it took the king of the walled city to cross," said Pali, looking down it.

"We cannot take the horses," said Arzu.

She and Pali looked at one another. Their horses were the finest in the land, save their mother's; and it was said their tribe loved their horses more than life itself. "More than life, but less than our sister," said Pali, as she unsaddled her dapple-grey, and was grateful for the veils that hid her tears.

Arzu rearranged her bundles: a carpet, a store of skeins, the ivory dagger, the jade stone with the hole in it, and some food. Pali bore nothing but the knotted message, the blue scarf, the three stones her sister had given her, and under her veils the golden comb.

They bid their horses return to the sphinx—either passage to grazing or a quick death would be their lot—and then, with Arzu taking Pali's left hand, they entered the darkness of the depths of the mountains.

As the fire within her grew, Sardeet began to see the invisible.

She asked her husband what he was giving her one day, when for three days he had fed her something that looked like pistachios and tasted like heaven, and which left her drowsy and happy. The drowsiness was not new; she had taken to rising for her bath and breaking her fast, and then lying dreamily on her cushioned couch until the djinn carried her to her husband's throne-room, where he fed her and spoke spells over her womb.

He was exceptionally attentive to her body, refusing to let her walk if she had the merest hint of a yawn, pressing more djinn into service. She forgot sometimes whether she was in a passage of silence or of speech, for the fire seemed to be pulling her words into it, her thoughts, her emotions, her memories. Her curiosity was swallowed in the sheer momentousness of bearing a god.

He turned to her with surprise, as if he'd forgotten she could speak, and smiling, said, "They are pistachios."

They did not taste like pistachios, she thought. They tasted … different. More real. More themselves.

It was in the silence after that meal she saw the first woman.

The road down into the dark was smooth and wide, as befit the road for the dead, Pali thought; the gods would fly above the pit. She and Arzu walked down, not speaking. Arzu was agonizingly tense, and Pali wanted to tell her to calm down, but she knew her sister did not have the benefit of three years training with the Warriors of the Mountain, and she did not want to alert the guardians of the dark to their presence.

Still, drawn by living breath, they came.

From some dim custom from her human life, not yet swallowed by the fire within her, Sardeet remembered the desire for fresh air. She struggled her way up to the tower. The djinn were forbidden the heights, and the silver wind did not leave her rooms, so Sardeet went up the last stairs alone and on foot.

At the top of the stairs, crouched in the corner of last turn, huddled a woman.

Sardeet stopped. The fire within her shifted, and she felt something else move in her that she could not name.

It was a day of her silence. Sardeet could not speak, could not make so much as a whimper or a moan of pleasure, could not laugh or snort or click her teeth. Even her bare feet were silent on the blue glass.

The woman sat with her knees drawn up and her face down. Her black hair spilled loose across her body, four feet or more in length, far longer than Sardeet's unbound. She wore loose green trousers and a long green tunic, of silk figured all over with sinuous embroidery in darker greens.

Sardeet stood before her at the top of the stairs, panting soundlessly, the fire in her belly throbbing counterpoint to her heartbeat.

At last the woman looked up. Her skin was lighter than Sardeet's, more bronze than copper, and her eyes slanted and almond-shaped. She was as beautiful, and in her black eyes Sardeet saw a light that she could almost put a name to, and tears of a grief that reached out and clenched around her heart.

For the first time since she had first eaten Olu-olurin's food she felt something with her whole heart.

The fire in her leaped up and then twisted away from the grief, as if it was anathema to the god growing within her, and Sardeet spasmed into a silent cry and collapsed on the stairs.

When at last she could look up the woman was gone.

At first it was just the clicking.

Pali and Arzu had walked hand in hand along what did not feel like a slope, but a straight road; they could see the golden circle of light far ahead of them but it illuminated nothing, merely blinded them.

From the sides and behind came the *tik-tik-tik* of many chitinous feet. Arzu squeezed Pali's hand very tightly. In her left hand she was readying the circlet she had knotted for the sphinx, and below her breath she murmured some of the words of power she had learned in the long nights at the monastery.

Pali drew from inside her robes the piece of gold pyrite. It was about the size of her fist, and had several pointed crystal extrusions. She drew out the sash and gave it to Arzu, who pried her fingers loose from her sister's. Murmuring prayers Arzu knotted one end about Pali's wrist and the other about her own, so that when they released each other's hands they had about four feet between them.

There were, so it was said in the stories, two scorpion-men for each day of the journey below.

Sardeet did not ask Olu-olurin about the woman. She asked instead about the pistachios.

"They are ordinary," he said in aggravation, with an expression that said her interruption was decidedly unwelcome. As her belly grew rounder he had stopped paying much attention to her head. Now she had to feed herself from the plates he brought, while he knelt beside her naked body and drew designs on her skin with paints and other substances. She was growing less hungry for food by the day, but the pistachios were still something she could taste.

But she had asked where exactly they came from, and he was obliged to tell her, so after he had finished muttering an incantation over her—it felt like settling into the bath of a morning, except for being fire—everything he did now was fire, accompanied by clouds of sacred incense—she waited patiently, eating the entire vast bowl of pistachios, until he said, "Fine! They come from Oclaresh! Are you satisfied?"

And, of course, she was silent. He smiled at her with an almost-human satisfaction in her silence, and bent back to his incantations over the god in her womb.

Over his shoulder she saw the second woman.

The scorpion-men came first from the left, to Arzu the weaver. They soon found they did not like the touch of the knots on their legs, for they felt the triple pull and push of the human paradox as an assault against their very being. They were guardians of the dead, built of the dead, fashioned out of giant insects and men who had fallen into grievous sin long ago when the world was another place.

To have a sudden tug of human mercy, or love, or artistic passion, when all was grim and stable and dark, would, Arzu acknowledged, be quite difficult.

~

The second woman was from the south, dark-skinned and with crinkled hair in elaborate braids. She was taller than Sardeet and thick-limbed and looked for a moment like a panther—Sardeet remembered, with a flash of pain and another silent spasm, her sister Arzu.

Olu-olurin looked up in disgruntlement. "Be still," he snapped. "I shall have to begin again."

Sardeet looked at him with wide eyes, trying to feign a passion she no longer felt, and his own glance met hers with an answering desire. She had not realized how much he had become entwined with her, nor did she know that between her human beauty and the divine power growing in her, he could barely contain his eagerness for her. He found her most desirable when silent, especially when she lay in one of his drowsy enchantments.

He was only going to give her the fruit that softened her waking mind, but she looked at him with such invitation that he forgot himself in the instant and began instead to shower her with his own kisses.

In the midst of this he ate some of the fruit from her own mouth, and when he had satisfied himself, he lay back amongst the clutter of their meal and slept.

Sardeet looked for the second woman, to see her gesture: *come*.

~

Pali, on the other hand, held a piece of iron pyrite the size of her fist, and when she hit the scorpion-men she created light.

The woman led her back to her own rooms. Sardeet had not called the djinn to her, instead panted along slowly, feeling drowsy and unwieldy and undeniably curious.

The woman stopped before the mirror. Sardeet, as ever, looked first at the glowing fire within her, and wondered what manner of god it would be, and how it would come forth. She had mostly stopped looking at herself, finding the change in her shape disconcerting. When she did meet her own glance in the mirror she sometimes felt she could see the fire rising up behind her eyes.

Now she looked. The woman beside her had no reflection. Sardeet herself stood there, her face radiantly beautiful (more beautiful than it had been; even she noticed), her eyes heavy-lidded, the designs Olu-olurin had painted on her looking like the intricate knotting of a carpet design. Her skin was coppery though she had been so rarely in the sun, and lit from within like glass.

Sardeet turned her head with difficulty to see the woman pointing impatiently at the mirror. Her face was beyond impatient, was twisted with a grief as strong and dowsing as the woman on the tower stair. Sardeet cried out silently, reaching to touch her, but though the woman stood at her side her hand passed straight through without resistance.

Pain seared through her. She doubled up around her great belly, and the silver wind caught her before she fell. Sardeet had a sudden memory of watching a horse foal with her sisters, and before she drank what the djinni brought to her she uttered a silent prayer in her heart for them.

In the absolute dark and silence after the screeching and the sparks and the chitinous horror, while Arzu shuddered and twisted at the end of the sash binding them, like a kite snagged by a falcon, Pali said, "Two."

～

Incredibly, she grew bigger.

Olu-olurin came now to her rooms, and she did not leave them, could not go more than a few dozen steps without flagging. He fed her again with his own hands, and rubbed ointments over her body, and gave her drinks and sweetmeats and sang incantations, and in her womb the fire burned ever hotter.

When she sat in the bath, the water steamed and bubbled around her.

She could not bear the touch of any cloth for long. She spent her days in the bath on Olu-olurin's suggestion, the djinn replacing the steam with cold water. She bade them sing when her husband was not there, the strange songs of the djinn that she'd tried to learn at the beginning of her sojourn. In the water, with the scented steam rising about her, the ethereal voices singing of inhuman things, the fire glowing through her skin, she could believe she was transfiguring into a goddess.

～

"Seven."

～

She had entirely lost track of how long she had been there, how long pregnant, how long she might yet have to bear this uncanny burden. In the mornings when the djinn lifted her from her couch, the silver wind whirling about her, she would go stand before the mirror. Every morning she told herself she would examine the mirror for what the woman had been trying to show her.

~

"Seventeen."

~

Every morning her glance drifted down and she stood in smiling adoration of the fire within her, until Olu-olurin came. His touch alone of all things was cool, and she welcomed him eagerly.

~

"Twenty-four," said Pali, as the last scorpion-man fell over with a ringing crash onto the stone, taking her pyrite with it. She shook her hand free of the vibrations and to loosen the tightness that had come with clenching the stone so long.

Arzu whispered, "In the dark. With only a stone."

Pali said, "I have two more, my sister," and tucked Arzu's hand in her arm, and together they walked up the slope to the circle of gold.

4

―――――

O ne night she woke to see arrayed about her bed six women.

Sardeet had lost track of what were dreams and what waking sensation. In both the fire was growing heavy, and recently—she did not know how recently—it had begun to speak to her. It did not speak in any words she understood, and its voice was neither male nor female, and its rhythm followed a distant beat she could not comprehend. But she had learned something, in her questions and her answers, about the Wind Lords, and she knew that comprehension was not what they required. Only obedience, and desire, and worship.

For the god in her womb, whispering like the softest wind over the sand in her mind, she felt love.

When they looked at each other in the sunlight on the other side of the passage, Pali saw that Arzu now had hair entirely silver. Arzu saw that Pali had white spots up her arm, and wondered what lay hidden beneath her veils.

Neither asked the other what she saw. Instead they turned and saw before them the Great Desert of Kaph, stretching in a level golden plain to the horizon where the winds were gathering a sandstorm to meet these intruders.

The fire seemed to be drawing everything of hers to feed its insatiable growth. She stroked her belly along the lines of the inscriptions Olu-olurin made, which did not wash off however long she stayed in the bath watching the water boil around her. She woke in the dark sometimes to see him standing over her, murmuring, glowing with his own power. She slept sometimes to have him walk in her dreams, still murmuring, raising passions that were never consummated but instead consumed by the fire.

She woke again in the light, and he was kneeling at her side, his voice unwavering, his attention entirely distant from her.

She smiled at her belly, listening to the inner voice growing stronger and yet lovelier, a counterpoint to Olu-olurin's chanting. She was drowsy and languidly pleased, lying on the cool glass—she could no longer bear any touch of cloth, anything but the glass, and the water, and his hand. One of the djinn brought her food, but she was no longer hungry, turned her head away. As she lay on her back on the floor her belly rose up before her like a tethered moon.

She blinked, and it was night, and Olu-olurin still knelt beside her, still chanting, and still the fire grew.

He paused, and as her eyes closed again, she said: "What will that achieve?"

And he said, reaching up to stroke her face and breasts with a hand that no longer felt cool: "Power."

She smiled, and no longer needed any potion or food to drift away to the contemplation of what glory grew in her womb, nor his incantations to open the door to her mind so that the god could learn power over men.

~

Pali saw the crevasse before Arzu stepped in it. When Arzu stopped at her touch, Pali knocked a pebble in. It made no sound as it fell.

"It is only a handswidth across," Arzu said.

Pali had her eyes closed. "I feel the wind," she replied; "it is blowing like the wind off the glaciers."

Arzu looked down at the crack at their feet, and drew out two skeins of thread: one blue as the sky or the scarf binding them, the other yellow as the sand in the distance before them. She chose two threads of the blue and two of the yellow, and braided them in an intricate pattern broken by careful knots. She then tied it very carefully to the jade stone Pali handed her, and laid it across the crevasse.

The jade weighted down the far side. On the nearer side she tied it to an outcropping of the black rock of the mountains. Over the crack, a pace across, stretched a ribbon wide as a finger.

Arzu went first, and Pali behind her, step by step, for seven days.

~

Sardeet woke to see Olu-olurin still kneeling beside her, but no longer chanting. He had lost his human seeming at some point, was now entirely blue, skin, hair, fingernails. Sardeet had not tried to think for a long time, but some old memory of a story stirred in her. The Wind Lords had their ranks, she knew. The highest were invisible. The lowest—

The fire flared, and she shifted position slightly. When she opened her eyes Olu-olurin had disappeared again.

Behind where he'd been in a semi-circle stood the six women, and all stared with horror except for one, the one in green, who looked at Sardeet with compassion and the grief that twisted her heart so.

She blinked, and Olu-olurin was giving her the tiny spoonful of the tears of the god, and as she swallowed the only food that had passed her lips for weeks, he smiled at her with that inhuman smile and said, "Soon."

At the edge of the holy desert, Pali and Arzu laid out their bait.

"It is said," said Arzu, "that the great eagles know the speech of men."

"Yes," said Pali, and across the carpet that Arzu had spread on the sand before them, she placed the gypsum rose. Arzu laid down the bridal circlet. After a moment, Pali added the message knotting, with its emblem of *blood calls to blood in need*, and Arzu placed the weeping statuette upon it. She and Arzu were still bound together by the blue scarf.

"It is said also," said Arzu, "that they know curiosity."

"Yes," said Pali, and moved the stone over slightly so it sat upon a black background.

"It is said also—"

"Hush," said Pali, who had glanced upwards, "the eagle comes."

Sardeet woke in a dream of an oasis to find that the six women were trying to touch her.

They could not touch her, of course; they were invisible, intangible, of the spirit world. Yet she was passing more and more into that world herself, and though some time ago she had felt nothing when she moved her hand through one of the women's forms, now their efforts felt like cool water.

She smiled, and groaned silently, though she did not remember what question she had asked her husband, what answer she had received. Perhaps it was still the same day since she had asked what he was working with his incantations.

The women would not leave her alone. Each time she started to slide away from consciousness, into the half-dreams where the fire had swallowed her entirely until she became a creature of the air like a free djinn of the holy desert, or the other half-dreams where she sat cradling a child, both of them entirely human, except that his eyes were fire, they touched her.

Finally she pushed herself up to her feet. She could not remember the last time she had stood. She swayed a little with dizziness, The god in her womb sang to her of beauty. She stumbled towards the mirror, drunk on the power within her, ready to look at her god from that other reflection and adore.

The women stood in front of the mirror. Sardeet tried to push them away, but though each brush of her hand through their bodies made them shudder, they crowded ever closer. She stumbled a step forward, looking for the mirror, pushing dumbly against the thickest cluster of ghosts. She couldn't make a sound, not even groan in exasperation. She could only push against what felt like thick cool air, until she realized she did not stand before the mirror, but had been led to its back.

The eagle was huge: certainly big enough to carry them, one in each talon. It landed on the sand before them, and stood looking, with first one eye and then the other. Pali saw herself reflected, and wondered what the eagle thought of the human women before him.

Arzu knelt as she had for the sphinx. "Lord of eagles," she said, "we are two sisters seeking our sister, and we beg you to help us."

The eagle had a very yellow beak; its nostrils were lined in orange. Its feathers were a rich bronze, catching gold in the sunlight. Arzu yearned to weave a carpet showing its magnificence. Pali wondered what it ate.

"Why?" said the eagle. "I have my own kindred."

The back of the mirror was not silver, as were the hand-sized mirrors Sardeet had seen in the world-without. It was made of a sleek grey stone, which even unpolished caught reflections of the light in her eyes and her womb.

Sardeet was not looking for her reflection, however. The women were still touching her, smothering her, pushing down the fire that had nearly consumed her. She could think clearly, at least a little.

In the middle of the stone was a keyhole.

Arzu said, "These are our offerings to you, lord of eagles."

"Little enough," said the eagle, and clenched one claw after another in the sand. "What blood is it that gives birth to a god? What marriage that is consummated in fire? What little desert stone that compares with a palace all of glass?"

He had not told her the punishment for opening that door.

"There is injustice here," said Pali, "and we come to avenge it."

The keys were on the other side of the room, beside the bed she had not slept in for so long she'd half-forgotten its purpose. Yet when she knelt to pick up the keys she rested her hands on a cushion a while before she could push herself up, and was immediately lost again in the fire.

In her dreams, she asked Olu-olurin what god her child would be, and he laughed and said: "Mine."

"I am listening," said the eagle, formally.

She woke with a voice calling her name fading away in her ears, running out of her body in a huge rush of loss. She opened her eyes to see nothing but the spirit women crowding her, plucking at her hair, her skin, her hands, all to waken her. They were nearly solid today.

"My name," she said aloud, so she must not have asked Olu-olurin about the god. "Where is my name?"

The women moved in greater urgency, the panic in their movements and expressions strong enough to reach through the fire. Sardeet grabbed the keys and was at first unable to push herself up. Finally she pushed herself on her rear to a glass pillar, which she was able to use to lever herself up. As she pulled the glass groaned.

All the palace seemed to ring in sympathy. Sardeet

panted loudly and then, with two spirit women under her arms as if trying to keep her upright, and the others dashing before her and the front of the mirror, she went to the back and the stone door with the keyhole for the golden key.

Her tears running down her face into her lips tasted like the god's.

~

"It is no injustice for the Wind Lords to take as a bride or a bridegroom one on their vision quest," said Arzu. "This is why they go arrayed in their wedding-clothes, in case they prove worthy. For their beauty, they are given the life immortal."

"So it is," said the eagle.

~

The key turned easily, and opened a third door to Olu-olurin's workroom.

~

"Our sister," said Pali, "weeps. We have come to right that wrong."

~

This time, Sardeet could see the invisible.

~

"It may be," said the eagle, "that it is an affront to the gods and not to mortals."

"It may be," replied Arzu, "but in the world the gods are accustomed to acting through men."

"Love I see here and grief," said the eagle. "And grief I see and love in the aerie above."

~

There were the books, and the table full of flasks where he made his ointments, and the wall of ingredients.

And there, hanging on the wall on six hooks, where she had seen only his magic cloaks — for invisibility, he'd said, kissing her; for disguise; for the shapes of other beings; and three days she had been silent, and content—were the bodies of six women.

Each of them looked deflated. Each of them had a rip in her belly. And there was, Sardeet saw, a seventh hook.

"Soon," he was muttering, pouring one liquid into another liquid. "Soon. And *this* time—seventh time—yes."

The ghosts were pushing her back, and Sardeet tiptoed as quietly as she could manage—not as quietly as she could under his silence—but he did not turn—she closed the door in the mirror softly.

~

"I will take you," said the eagle.

~

When she lifted the key from the lock her hand was covered in blood.

5

The eagle carried them one in each taloned foot. It had permitted them to undo the scarf binding them, but the offerings they left to it or to the gods or the djinn. It carried them not out into the desert—like their sister they were surprised—but straight up the face of the mountains, to a palace of blue glass that caught the sunlight like a mirage, but whose door opened to the eagle.

It flew inside a vast hall to a throne made of a silvery blue glass, and set them down before it before flying out again. Once the sound of its wings faded there was no sound at all.

Arzu said softly to Pali, "The opal."

Pali gave it to her, and Arzu took out a thread of green, which had been Sardeet's favourite colour, and tied it around the stone with a special knot. She played out about an ell of thread before cutting it with the ivory dagger. She offered the dagger to Pali, who shook her head and displayed her open hands. Arzu remembered then that the injustice was to be righted without use of weapons, that the Warrior might prove herself worthy of a sword.

Once she let the opal hang loose they waited. Pali now

had nothing but the golden comb in her hair. Arzu had in her bundle only her skeins of thread and the dagger.

The glass around them suddenly emitted a noise like a soft bell. Pali turned to Arzu to see that the opal dangling in her hand had started to move.

They followed its gentle swinging. Each time they came to an intersection—and there were many, the palace was a maze of curving walls and interconnected rooms—they paused to see which way the opal moved. Pali had seen dowsers at work looking for the hidden springs, and knew the knot that tied the opal, but not the braid in the thread that made the knot.

They wound through the blue rooms. None of the openings afforded a glimpse to anything besides more cool blue glass. No sight of the outside, no art or fabric within, nothing but room after room of cool empty glass.

The fire in her had started to move. At first it expanded, pushing away all thoughts of fear or even pain, and then, as it contracted suddenly to a tiny spot below her womb, every tiniest portion of her body, inside and out, came alive and into full consciousness of agony. Sardeet dropped the keys and tried to rub at her hand with the other. She kept missing across the huge expanse of her belly.

On the second expansion she made it halfway to the bath, but the contraction caught her and she fell to the ground in agony, and once down she could only lie flat.

Olu-olurin came in and stood over her, with the flask in his hand. His eyes roved over her body with great pleasure, and when he saw the blood on her hand he grinned.

"We did not speak of the penalty for opening that door," he said.

She felt the expansion rising up in a storm of euphoria, but before it could engulf her again she managed to ask: "What *are* you?"

He smiled and kissed her on the lips as the euphoria catapulted her briefly into divinity before the contraction pulled her back down into bitter humanity.

"I thought you would never think to ask," he said.

At an intersection where seven rooms led off at angles to each other, the opal stopped. It refused to move even when Arzu swung it. They looked at the silent palace around them, trying to hear any sound of habitation.

"It's a maze," said Arzu. "We're lost." She began to unwind her last long skein, but then Pali said—"There—I see someone—" and started running. Arzu hastily followed, seeing nothing but a flash of green amidst all that blue and hoping it was not just a trick of the light.

"I am Lord of the Blue Wind now," said Olu-olurin. "I was a wizard of the City of Enchanters, half djinni and half human. I was beautiful: taken as a consort by one of the Wind Lords. She was gentle, did not bind me, came to love me. Over time bent to me, bowed to me, was swallowed by me, as the little whirlwind by the greater. I made a bargain with one of the devil-kindred for knowledge beyond the lot of a little wind."

Sardeet could not speak, since he had begun to answer her question, but he seemed to know her thoughts, for he kissed her nose.

"Those in the desert? The Twelve work through men and lesser spirits. My fellows of the lesser winds? They have their own concerns, their own searches … to become one of the Twelve is a long and arduous task. A thousand years I have been studying the ways. Oh, the things I have learned. I am half djinni; I have through my disciplines destroyed the mortal part of me. Thus far a Wind Lord. But I am of human kindred: not *truly* immortal. Not one of the Twelve. That comes another way."

He caressed her body, running his hands over the designs on her belly that were now nearly etched into her skin. She shuddered with mingled desire and fear, and he smiled at her.

"I have learned the ancient secrets. I have discovered new ones. I learned how I could bring those mortal women nearly towards divinity. The tribes send out their most beautiful to be brides to the winds, if we choose. I live at the edge of the desert, that I might choose first. The Blue Wind, lover of beauty. I will be one of the Twelve, and beautiful as you, fire as you, alive immortal. The seventh body will be mine, the fire in its heart my soul. The Twelve admire beauty best of all. When I take upon me our child's body they will call me home."

∿

Pali ran after the green figure only to have it disappear on her, but by then she had heard a voice speaking. She crept forward to see what had befallen.

∿

Sardeet opened her eyes to see that the ghost women had left her, all but the one in green, who stood anxiously until Sardeet looked at her. Sardeet could barely think through her horror and her desire, but nodded.

Olu-olurin whipped around but the ghost had vanished. Sardeet felt the wave of euphoria expanding in her. The fire in her was spreading—she could feel it nearly ready to spring forth—

"Each time I refined it. Each time I realized that what I needed was to refine myself, my body." He stroked her belly eagerly. "I impregnated my wives. Enchanted them, enhanced them, broke the chains of their humanity until they became worthy vessels. At the rebirth left the old husk for the new glory, each time with more fire, less clay. Each time one step closer. *This* time your beauty was so divine already that I think—this time is enough."

His hunger was so naked she turned from him and as the contraction seized her retched liquid fire across the floor.

This room was still all cool blue glass, but there were cushions in a smattering of colours off to one side, and what Pali took to be a cistern in the centre of the room. A huge mirror to the left reflected them; instinctively she stepped to one side to be out of its view.

Between the mirror and the cistern stood a man who looked as if he'd been shaped out of the same glass as the walls—all blue, naked, and with a strange flame running inside him. He had been speaking. He leaned forward to kiss the figure before him.

One of their mother's most prized possessions was an alabaster jar she had won from some caravan long ago. It was simple, without carved ornamentation, but its lines were perfect enough to draw tears from an unwary soul. On special feasts their mother placed a candle within it, and it glowed like the divine idea of beauty.

That was what Arzu thought, seeing her sister, and she heard no words.

Pali listened to the blue man explain himself, and saw that he seemed fair set to rape her sister—marriage or not she could see no consent left there—and as she saw that she saw the light in Sardeet suddenly wink out, and her sister collapsed across the floor with a trickle of fire coming from her mouth.

~

In Sardeet's mind, the soft voice of her child said, *"Name me."*

~

Pali did not wait; she had been trained not to wait, once the decision was made. She let out a wild yell of warning, and as the blue Wind Lord turned in shock she had already landed upon him, and bore him skidding across the floor. Arzu ran to kneel beside Sardeet, pulling her yarns apart until she could disentangle the circlet she had made before the sphinx.

"Sardeet," she said, wrapping her sister's hands in an intricate looping, tying on additional strings, knotting the special patterns that she had been taught by her grandmother in the women's tent before she went to learn from the carpet makers.

"Sardeet."

~

She was finally cold, but the fire was all around her. She felt languid, delighted, unable to be afraid. She tried to think. This was not her husband reincarnate; this was the voice she had been hearing all these months. She would not let her husband take this god away from the world.

~

"Sardeet. Sardeet-savarel. Sardeet."

Pali crashed Olu-olurin straight into the mirror, and shattered it all over the floor. Scarlet blood spilled out across the blue glass, and some high keening rose out of the strange whispering silences of the palace.

Over by the bath, Arzu cut the last string of her working.

In her deepest contraction yet, Sardeet found a voice in her mind, and: "*Arvoliin,*" she said; *Flame of the Fire of Love.*

When Sardeet named her child the air in the room seemed to catch fire. All four of them stopped, waiting: Pali sitting on Olu-olurin, her hands around his neck, not quite completing the twist. Arzu kneeling beside Sardeet, her hands on the web keeping her sister human. Olu-olurin's black eyes glittering with an emotion without a name. Sardeet, curled around her enormous belly, listening.

All of them heard the god say, "*Now.*"

Sardeet cried out in silent agony, her body arcing off the ground, her face blazing out of pain into ecstasy. Arzu pulled her last length of thread, pure gold, and when her sister arced a second time and gave birth in a great fountain of fire, it was she who received the newborn god into her hands and used the gold thread to cut the cord of fire that seemed his umbilicus.

Her hands were steady, though Arzu's face was as twisted

with pain and wonder as those of the ghost women she could not see who stood beside her.

Pali's arms contracted in fear and wonder and fury, and the snap of Olu-olurin's neck breaking echoed loud.

Before the sound had died the god had lost his infant form, and stood there before them a winged flame. They stared.

He spoke to Arzu: "Be wise"; to Pali, "Be joyous"; to the last momentary glimpse of Olu-olurin, "Repent"; to the six dead women, "Be at peace"; and to his mother, "Beloved."

And then he was gone.

Pali dropped the corpse of her sister's husband upon the floor. She felt the need to say something, but could think of nothing that was remotely appropriate.

"Never once," said Sardeet, "did he ask me my name."

"That was ill done of him," said Arzu.

"He killed six wives before me."

"That was even less well done of him."

"He accidentally fathered a god."

Arzu paused judiciously. "Perhaps it was that you mothered one."

"He will call you home one day," Pali said softly, and Sardeet began again to cry, though now her tears were salt.

It took six months for Arzu to knot a new carpet from the threads she found in the palace, and that was with both Pali and Sardeet helping unravel the fabric of cushions and clothes. Arzu worked beside Sardeet, who lay in her bed weak and chilled for long days, and sang to her the songs of their people, while Pali made an inventory of the treasure-room and considered what best to do.

It was a year and a day from the meeting at the crossroads that Pali and Arzu brought their sister Sardeet-savarel home from her marriage to one of the Wind Lords. She was not yet seventeen, and more beautiful than ever, though her face was grave and her attention seemingly turned to a distant sound, and people wondered if she had left part of her soul behind her in the holy desert. That she had done well in her marriage was an understatement; though people did wonder how it was that she could be widowed who had wed one of the gods.

That Arzu should have knotted a carpet that could fly even over the Black Mountains was considered a tribute to her skill and wisdom, and her new gravity—and the marker of the gods' touch in her untimely white hair—meant that the murmurs that she would become Queen after her mother's retirement displeased no one; though she herself was best pleased when she designed a carpet that finally captured something of the beauty of the lord of the eagles, and she achieved the second mastery.

People knew the stories about the Warriors of the Mountain. When they saw Pali dismount in her black veils, bearing no weapon, with her sister the new widow beside her, her cousins and clansmen backed away from both of them. For if Sardeet's beauty was fully worthy of a god's attention, it was surely Pali who had made her the god's widow.

After the mourning-feasts, Pali chose not to return to the mountains. Still dressed in the flowing black garments that were the First Veil, she took the best horse out of the line that had given her the dapple-grey, and with saddlebags full of the treasures of Olu-olurin, set out to return the bones of his dead wives to their homelands.

In the next ceremony of dedication, after Arzu presented her eagle carpet and after they burned the frankincense that Pali had sent from some far corner of the world by devious routes and terrified traders, the shamans caused to be engraved on the stele of the Oclaresh clansmen the name of the newest of the gods.

After her father finished the engraving, Sardeet put on widow's white and went walking in the desert to look for stones that might show her another path. She found a white rock sprouting with garnets, and jade of her favourite green, and another ingot of fool's gold, and she stood there for a long time before it occurred to her that the answers to her questions no longer lived in the wind, but in the world.

She was just seventeen when she went to the city.

AUTHOR'S NOTE

Thank you for reading!

The Bride of the Blue Wind begins the stories of the Sisters Avramapul, who will go on to many adventures by themselves and as part of the Red Company. *The Warrior of the Third Veil* continues their adventures and will be followed by *The Weaver of the Middle Desert* in 2022.

The Tower at the Edge of the World, which tells of the origins of another member of the Red Company, is currently available. *In the Company of Gentlemen*, a related story set many decades after *The Bride of the Blue Wind*, is also available.

You may also be interested in the Greenwing & Dart series, which begins with *Stargazy Pie*, and *The Hands of the Emperor*, which are set on different worlds within the same narrative universe.

You are welcome to visit my author website (www.victoriagoddard.ca) where you can buy books, get in touch, find out about new releases, and more.

www.ingramcontent.com/pod-product-compliance
Lightning Source LLC
Chambersburg PA
CBHW051236210726
48290CB00003B/988